Peter Curry

You and Me-Me

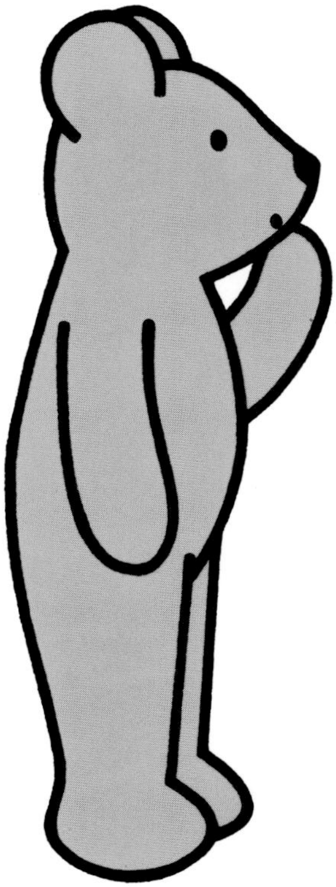

Published by Price/Stern/Sloan Publishers, Inc.
410 North La Cienega Boulevard, Los Angeles, California 90048

ISBN: 0-8431-1048-1

PRICE/STERN/SLOAN
Publishers, Inc., Los Angeles
1984

Hello! Are you down there?

You're not up here either, are you?

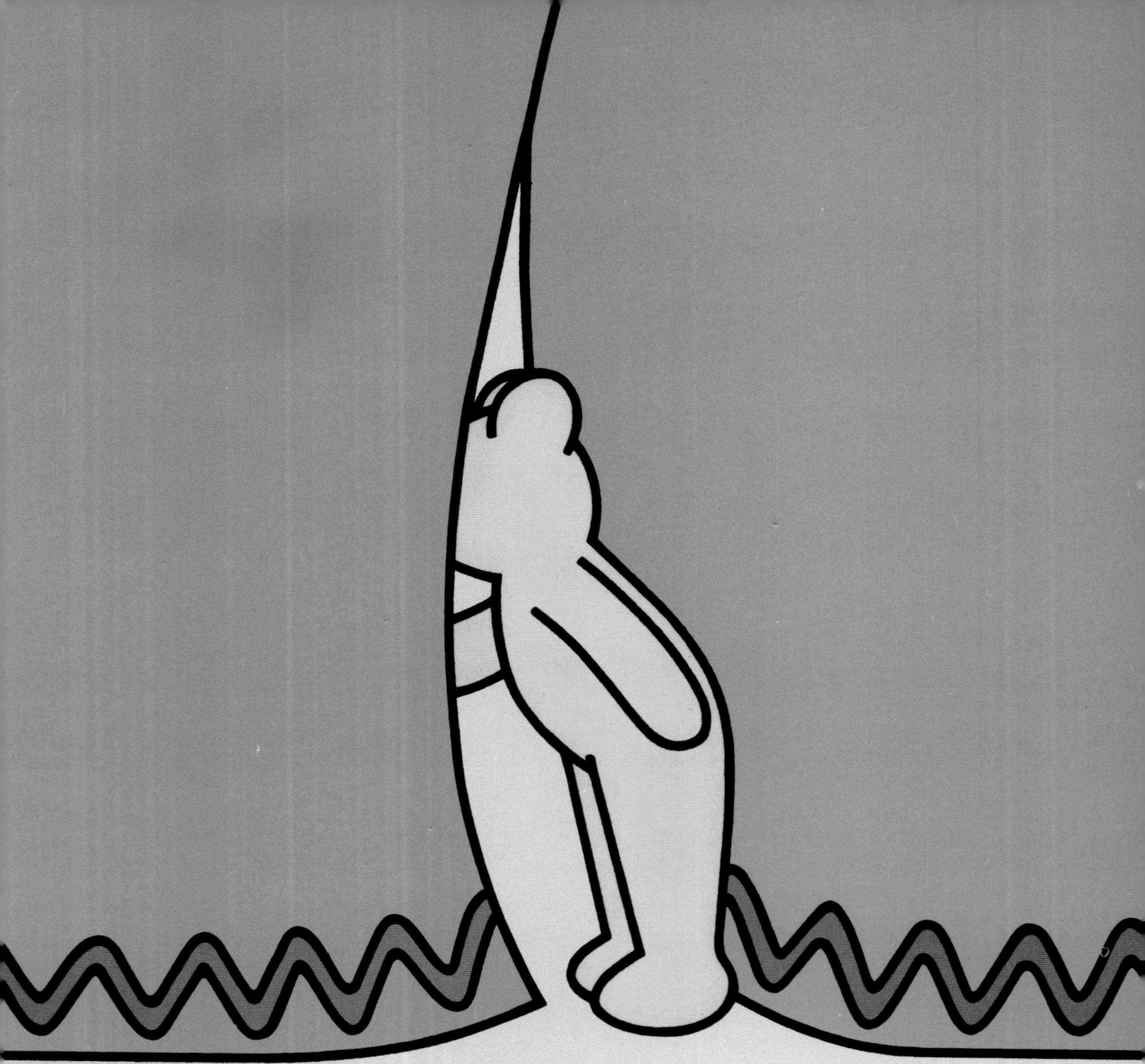

I know where you are.
You're hiding behind these curtains.
No! You're not there.

I can't find you anywhere!
Where can you be?

There you are! Hello!
My name is Me-Me,
because I always say that word twice.
What is your name?
Will you play with me-me?

Oh dear! I think I am going to sneeze, and if I sneeze – atchoo!

. . . . I become invisible –
until someone touches my nose!
Will you touch my nose?
Silly me-me. I forgot. I can see you –
but you can't see me-me!

I've fetched my umbrella and boots to help you see me-me. Can you touch where you think my nose should be?

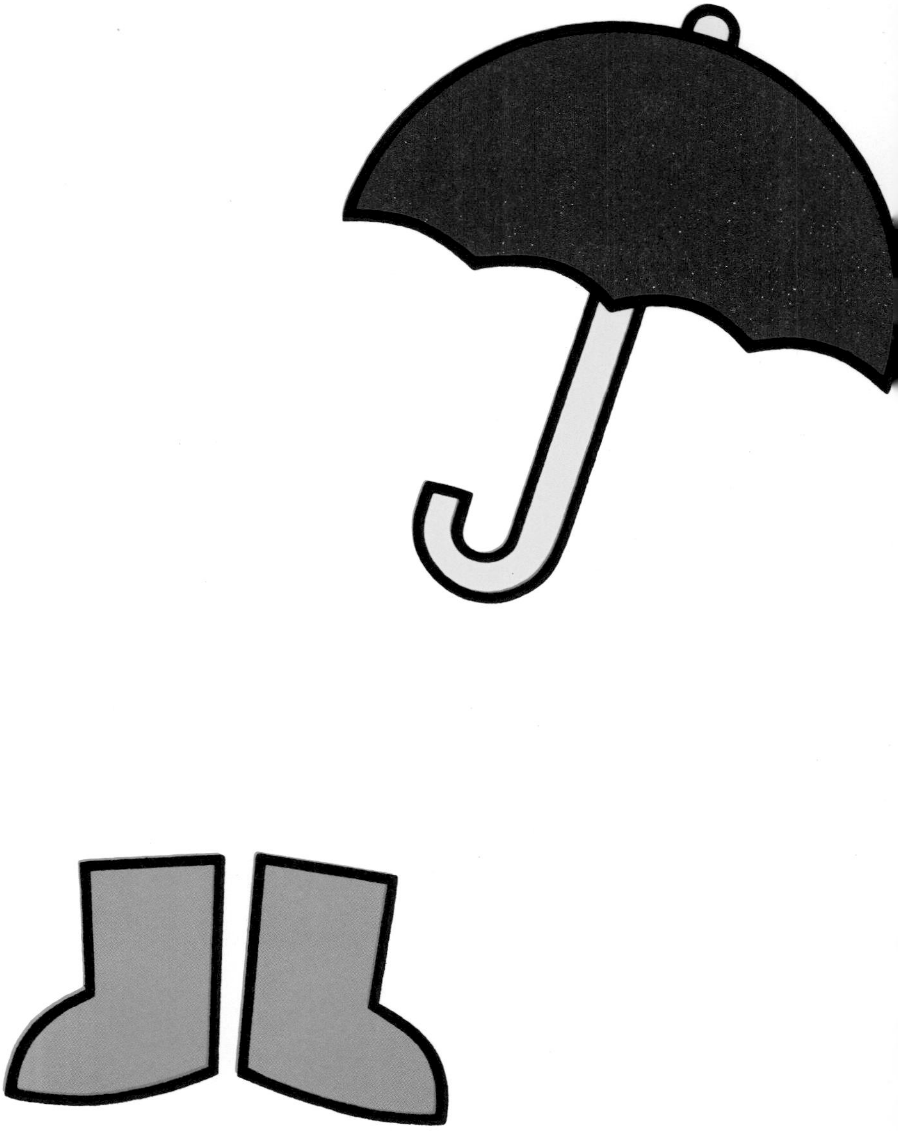

**Tee-hee! That tickled,
but you didn't quite touch my nose,
so I am still invisible.**

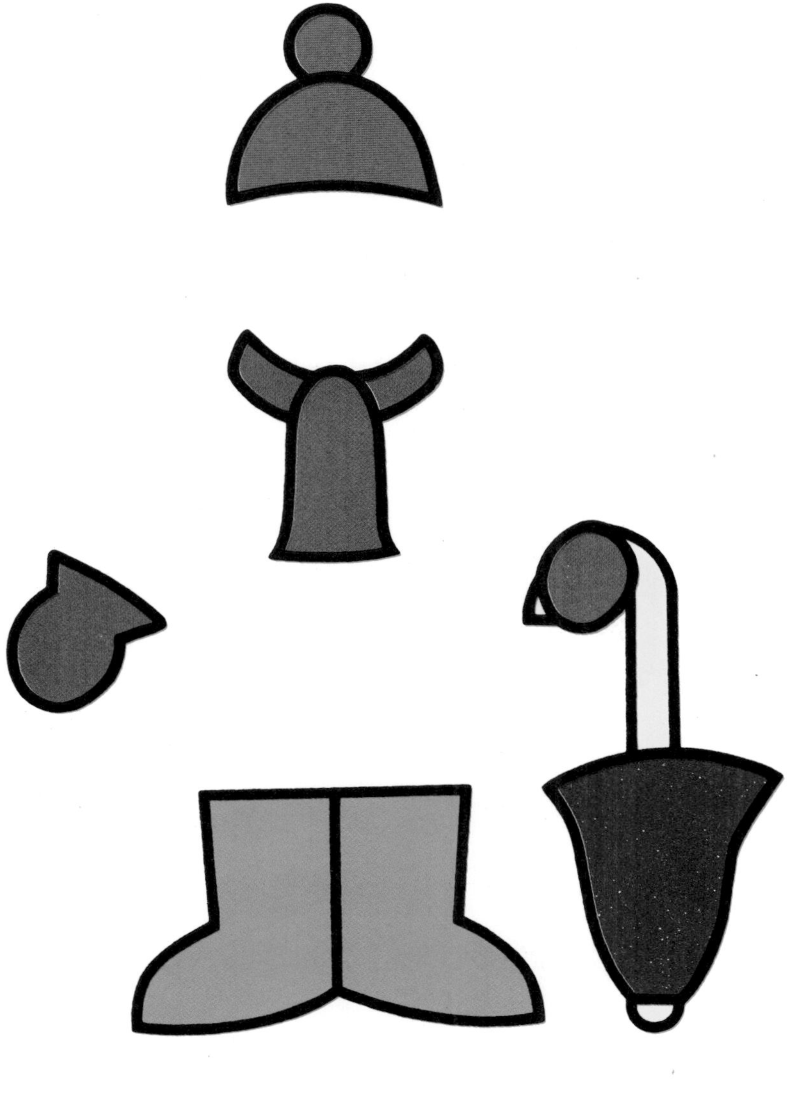

There! I've put on my hat and scarf and my mittens. Will you try again?

That's better. Thank you.
It isn't cold or raining
so I'll take these things home again.
Would you like to come with me-me?

Through the gate we go
and into the garden.

Can you find the way to my house, up the higgledy-piggledy path, without stepping over the grass?

**Here is my house.
It's rather odd – like the path.
Can you find what's wrong with it
while I just go inside?**

Here I am.
Would you like to come inside too?
Which door shall I open for you?
Will you choose a door to knock on?

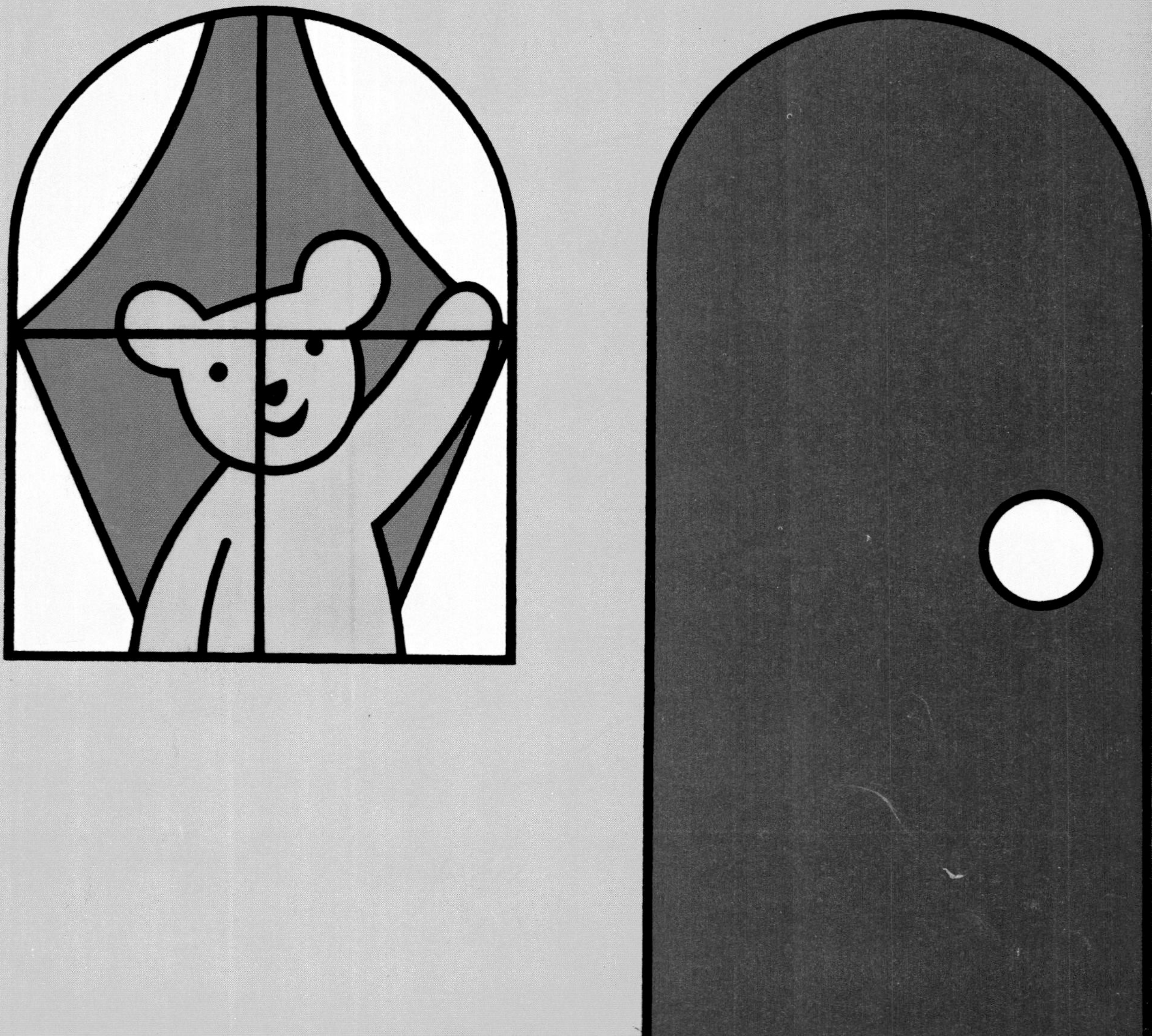

Hello. Come in.

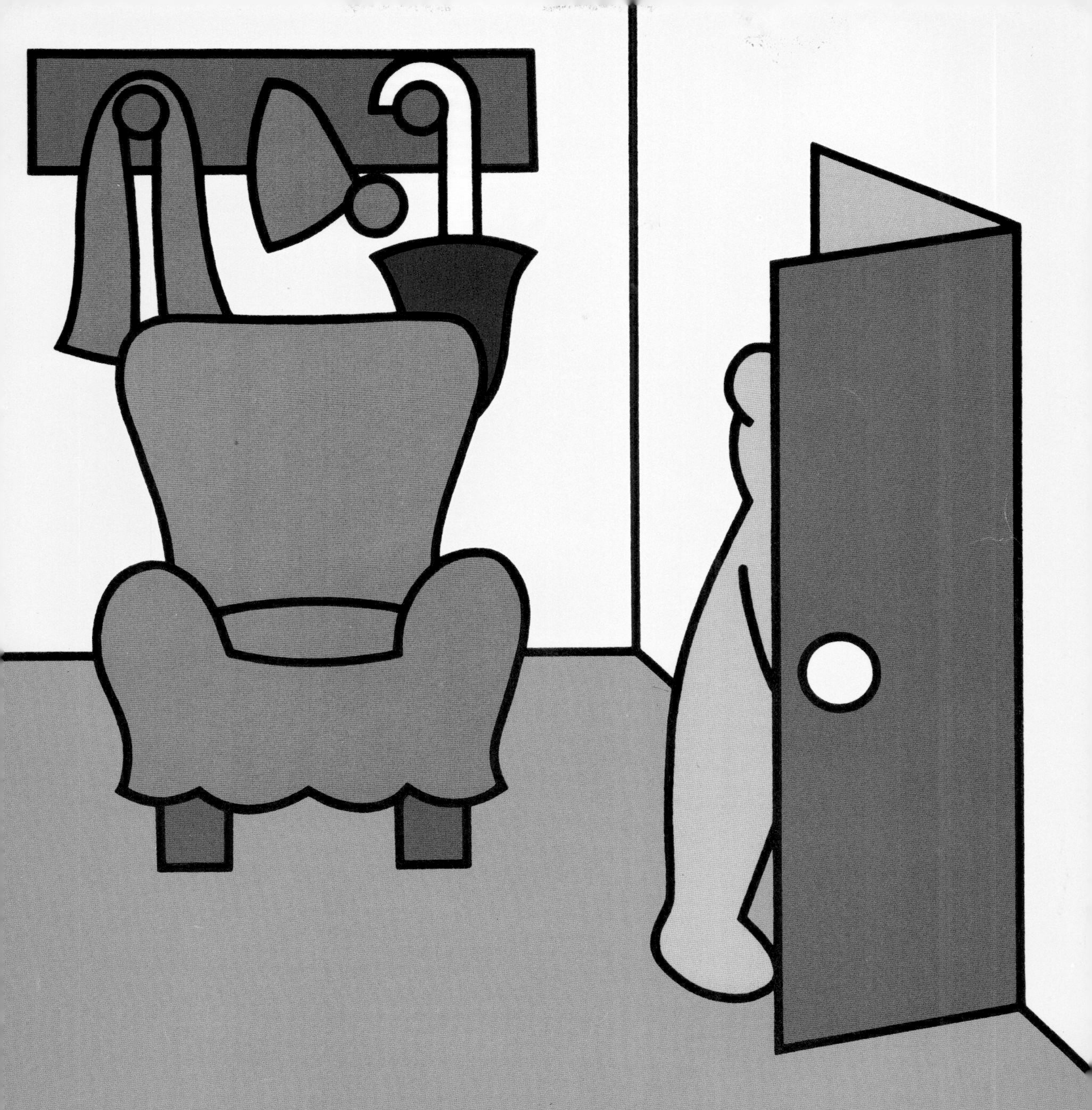

Here is my front room
and if we go through this door . . . .

. . . . we are in my bedroom.

Would you like to see inside my cupboard? There is something I want to show you!

I am looking for a yellow box.
Will you help me-me to find it?
I can't see it, can you?

**Let's take everything out
and put it all on the floor.
There's the box. Can you see it?
Guess what is inside.**

It's a camera – for taking pictures.
I press the button
and out pops the picture.
Shall I take your picture
in the garden?

Smile. Say cheese.
Now I press the button – Click!

Here is your picture.
It only shows your eyes and nose!
I was standing too close to you.
Will you take my picture now?

Can you see me-me
through the little window?
Press the button when I say cheese.
One – two – three – Cheese!

Here is the picture.
It's a good one, isn't it?

Just look at the time!
It's nearly two clouds past the sun!
I have two little jobs to do.

First I must water the flowers.
Can you guess what my other job is?

There! All finished.
I am so tired I think I might yawn,
and if I yawn – Oh . . . . .

. . . . I turn upside-down!
Will you turn me-me
up the right way, please?

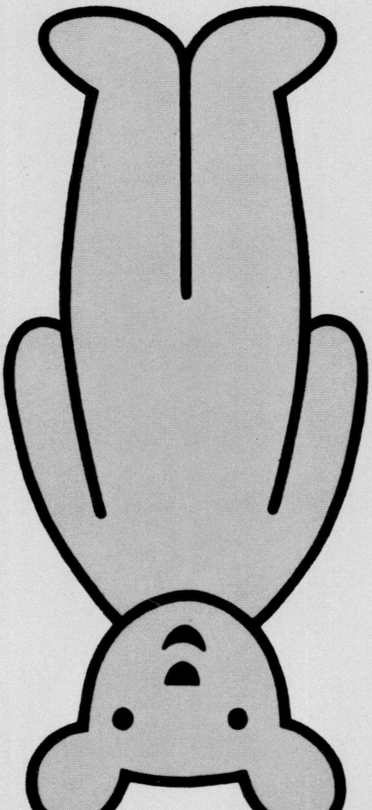

Thank you.
I think I will have a sleep now.
Will you come to see me-me
again soon? Bye-bye.